ANNABELLE'S
RED DRESS

BY LANI LUPUL

ILLUSTRATED BY ALLISON ANTONIO

To all the kids learning to use their voice.

Springtime begins again,
with fresh blooms all around.
And if I'm really quiet,
I hear them bursting from the
ground.

Flowers are so pretty,
with very little noise.
It's like someone taught them
how to use their little voice.

My name is Annabelle,
I am your little girl.
God trusted you and Mommy
to show me this big world.

These Daddy-daughter letters
show that love it does come plenty,
For in this home we live in,
my heart is never empty.

It's birthday breakfast time,
here comes my gift with a bow.
The red satin dress inside
makes me shine with a glow!

Then Daddy, you bent down,
with a smile upon your face,
Darling, this gift will teach you
that your voice has a place.

The heart is what matters,
not the dress that you wear,
So take these words with you,
as you learn how to care.

When trouble comes – and of course it will –
a strong wind from home will blow.
Look up, remember – a brave girl keeps going –
and courage you will show.

I forgot what you had said,
until that day at school,
When wearing something satin
made me feel pretty cool.

I showed off my red dress
and beamed my full-face smile.
It felt like I was loved
because of my new style.

But as the day went on,
my heart just cared too much.
I forgot all you had said –
that I am more than enough.

One by one all the kids
started to go their own way.
I guess that their cheering
didn't mean they would play.

Then a girl I never talk to
stood tall against my face.
She spoke angry words at me
that pushed my heart out of place.

Tears came bursting out,
and anger roared in me.
It seemed my day was ruined,
so I ran behind a tree.

As I huddled tight below,
I remembered what you said;
Then came a whooshing sound,
as words danced inside my head.

When trouble comes - and of course it will -
a strong wind from home will blow.
Look up, remember - a brave girl keeps going -
and courage you will show.

I shook the dust off my dress,
no longer feeling small.
Hands clenched with red satin,
I suddenly felt six feet tall.

The wind tickled my dress,
and I began to twirl.
Giggling and feeling brave,
I ran towards that angry girl.

Hey, you standing there,
with your hurtful tongue!
Well, it's my birthday,
and I am not going to run.

Though I'm smaller than you,
my heart has just grown.
Can we please try friendship,
before we both go home?

The mean girl started crying,
so I hugged her oh so tight.
She heard my caring voice
change the wrong into right.

Daddy, I chose your words,
with my head held high.
A brave girl keeps going
and will always try.

To love those who don't know
that they are doing wrong.
To be kind and help others
to sing a brand-new song.

My voice it just bloomed and
helped me find some friends.
Better than any red dress,
is how this birthday ends.

CPSIA information can be obtained
at www.ICGtesting.com
Printed in the USA
LVHW072056260321
682481LV00022B/4